This book belongs to

____

PETER COTTONTAIL'S SURPRISE

Illustrated by
GREG HILDEBRANDT

Story by
BONNIE WORTH

The Unicorn Publishing House
New Jersey

PETER COTTONTAIL'S SURPRISE

Once upon a time,
in the woods not very far from here,
there lived a young rabbit
with soft sandy-brown fur,
bright black eyes,
and the cutest little white
tufted tail you ever saw.
His name was Peter — as his father
and grandfather and great grandfather
and great *great* grandfather were named
before him. Peter Cottontail.

Peter Cottontail lived
beneath a clearing,
deep under the ground
where it is safe and cozy,
in a warren.
Peter was a lucky bunny
for the Cottontail Clan
was vast — and there was
always somebody to play with.
Well, almost always.

PETER COTTONTAIL'S SURPRISE

It was the very first day of Spring,
and, as you can well imagine,
Peter was feeling restless and frisky and eager to go outdoors as all little creatures are in the Spring, when the leaves are budding, the streams are bursting and the first wildflowers are beginning to make their rainbow across the meadow.

Peter Cottontail went to his mother and said, "Mama Cottontail, will you take me outside to see the Spring?"

"I can't right now, Peter Cottontail. I've got three split pea pies in the oven. Why not ask Great Grandpa Cottontail? His whiskers are just twitching to be up and out."

"Great Grandpa Cottontail," he said, "will you please take me up and show me the Spring?"

Great Grandpa Cottontail was whittling away at a fine piece of white oak.

"I can't right now, Peter Cottontail. I promised somebody I would make a present and I cannot go out until I have finished it."

"What present are you making?" Peter asked eagerly.

"Never you mind, Peter Cottontail. Run along and ask your Cottontail cousins. They are always the first to be out and running and batting at the daisies and the black-eyed susans."

So Peter Cottontail went to find his cousins.

Peter found one cousin in the storage tunnel.

"Shhh!" said his cousin, Lotty Cottontail.
"We're playing hide-n-seek."

Peter Cottontail looked around. Penny and Polly Cottontail were nowhere to be found.

"But Lotty Cottontail," Peter said, "it is Spring. Why are you running around down here when you could be up in the great wide world, running and leaping and batting at daisies and black-eyed susans?"

"Pah!" said Cousin Lotty. "Who needs it? Go ask your grandmother. She's been waiting all winter long to collect those old twigs of hers."

Peter Cottontail found his grandmother in her work room.

"Grandma Cottontail," he said, "I'd just love to go up with you and collect some winter twigs."

"Tut-tut, Peter Cottontail," Grandma Cottontail said. "My box is full of sticks. I went out this morning when the dew was still fresh and gathered them."

Poor Peter's ears drooped. "You mean I have missed the dawn? Goodness me! Who will take me outside before the first day of Spring is over?"

"That's a father's job," said Grandma Cottontail, "if you ask me."

Peter found his father up in the back hallway hard at work with Uncle Cottontail.

Father Cottontail stopped digging when Peter spoke. Brushing the damp dirt from his whiskers, he said, "I have no time to take you out, Peter Cottontail. Can't you see I've got to finish clearing out our back doorway?"

Peter Cottontail looked and saw that, indeed, winter storms had washed it nearly closed.

"I think there's just enough room," said Father Cottontail, "for a middle-sized bunny like yourself to squeeze through and greet the Spring."

Peter blinked. "All by myself?"

"I think you're old enough now," his father said.

Peter twitched his nose. "I think I smell it," he said. "I can! I can smell the Spring!" he cried.

Peter Cottontail squeezed and wiggled and dug his way out the back door. He stood stock still in the doorway, looking out on the new Spring. Only his whiskers moved.

"What do you see?" his father called up to him.

Peter Cottontail found his voice at last. "I see a bright yellow butterfly!" he said. "Oh, Father, it is the most perfect Spring day I have ever seen!"

His father laughed. "Run along now and play."

Peter Cottontail hopped out into the clearing and looked around at the daisies and the black-eyed susans, at the wild grape and the onion grass, at the blue sky and the new leaves and the butterflies flitting all around.

"This day is so perfect," Peter Cottontail said, "that I must find a friend to share it with me."

And he hopped off down the bunny trail in search of a friend.

When he had been hippety-hopping down the trail for quite some time, he came upon Squire Squirrel's tall oak tree.

"Squire Squirrel," Peter said, "can the squirrel kittens come out and play acorn hockey with me?"

"Goodness, no," said the Squire, "They have Spring chores to do and cannot play until they have finished."

"Oh," said Peter Cottontail, his ears drooping just the slightest bit. "Thank you, anyway." And he hopped off slowly.

Hippety-hopping a little further on, Peter Cottontail came to the stream, rushing clear and cool from the winter's thaw. Rutherford Raccoon sat on its bank, staring down into the water.

"Will you come play Leap-Bunny with me, Rutherford?" Peter asked.

Rutherford pulled his bushy salt-and-pepper tail around in front. "Does this look like a cottontail to you? I don't leap. I skulk and I fish and I climb and I sneak but I do not leap. Now run along before I miss a fat fish."

Ears drooping just a little bit more, Peter Cottontail went on his way.

Peter Cottontail was loping along when he spied Professor Porcupine sitting up in a tree, nibbling away at new leaves.

"Want to run a race, Professor?" Peter Cottontail asked.

"I am eating, Peter Cottontail," the professor said. "Kindly remember that it makes my bristles itch to run so soon after a meal."

Peter Cottontail was beginning to feel an itch all his own. A very special itch all over his body; the itch to run and leap and scamper and creep all through the Spring meadows that were just on the other side of that thicket of fir trees.

"If no one will play with me, I'll play by myself. If no one will run with me, I'll run by myself. For this is a perfect Spring day and my name is Peter Cottontail!"

Peter Cottontail burst into the open, running and leaping and racing through the pale rainbow of wildflowers stretching across the meadow.

"This is the most perfect day!" Peter Cottontail cried to the blue blue sky. "Even if I am the only creature in the forest who knows it!"

All of a sudden, Peter stopped and stood stock still.

Peter Cottontail's ears and whiskers both twitched at once. Only his soft sandy-brown fur and his beady black eyes were still. He was listening to a high sweet piping noise and it seemed to be coming from the clearing near his home.

"What could it be?" he wondered, and he set off in the direction of the wonderful sound.

Peter Cottontail hopped back through the meadow, back along the bunny trail, past Professor Porcupine's tree, past the stream where Rutherford had fished, past Squire Squirrel and the squirrel kittens' tree . . . and all the while, the piping music grew louder and clearer and sweeter.

Finally, Peter broke into the clearing near his home.

"SURPRISE!"

Surprise, indeed. Peter Cottontail was so startled that he fell plunk on his puffy cottontail.

"Happy birthday, Peter Cottontail,
Happy birthday, to you!"

Peter Cottontail looked around at all the Cottontail Clan and at all his woodland friends, "Why, I never even guessed!"

"Of course not!" they all said, for they knew how to keep a surprise. "Now open your presents, Peter Cottontail, for we are all starved."

As the sky deepened and the stars came out and the great round moon rose overhead, the animals feasted on woodland treats. Afterwards, they played games until the sky grew lighter and the moon began to sink.

"It's time for our Peter Cottontail to go to bed," said his mother and father.

Peter Cottontail went around and hugged each of his friends and relatives and thanked them for making such a wonderful surprise party. But he saved the biggest hugs for his mother and father.

"This is the most perfect day I've ever had. And you know what?" Peter Cottontail said. "Next time, I want to make the surprise."

The Unicorn Publishing House; 1148 Parsippany Blvd.; Parsippany, NJ 07054

Distributed in Canada by Doubleday Canada, Ltd., Toronto, ON, Canada

◆◆◆◆◆

Special thanks to Kate Klimo

◆◆◆◆◆

Designed and Edited by Jean L. Scrocco
Printed in Singapore by Singapore National Printers Ltd through Palace Press, San Francisco
Typography by TG&IF, Inc., Fairfield, NJ
Reproduction Photography by the Color Wheel, New York, NY

◆◆◆◆◆

Printing History 15 14 13 12 11 10 9 8 7 6 5 4 3

Library of Congress Cataloging in Publication Data
Main entry under title:

Hildebrandt, Greg.
Peter Cottontail's Surprise.

Summary: Peter Cottontail has a surprise birthday party.
1. Children's stories, American. [1. Rabbits — Fiction.] [2. Birthdays — Fiction] I. Worth, Bonnie. II. Title.
PZ7.H5456Pe 1985 [E] 84-28031
ISBN 0-88101-015-4